The King of Arcabuco

Written by Nadine Cowan

Illustrated by Nadine Cowan and Katie Crumpton

Collins

Chapter 1

Once Kisanu Hair and Beauty had opened its doors each morning, there wasn't a moment of silence until closing time. EJ and his cousin, Aniyah, had come to get their hair done. The clippers buzzed as Jamal gave EJ a shape-up, Yara spritzed her client's curls with leave-in conditioner, and three women chatted beneath the hairdryers. Kisanu was owned by EJ and Aniyah's aunt, and it was a few doors down from Blue Mahoes, Aniyah and EJ's family restaurant.

"Aniyah, do you know what style you want?" asked Aunt Joy.

Aniyah sunk into the salon chair. "No, Aunty."

"How about this?" Olivia pointed to an image in a glossy magazine. Olivia was Aniyah's best friend and she'd come to keep Aniyah company.

Aniyah shook her head. "That'll take forever."

"Hmm. Yes, you can never sit still for long!" Aunt Joy laughed.

"Why are they called canerows?" Olivia asked.

Joy thought for a moment. "Well, we've worn them for thousands of years, and they've been called by many names. The Yoruba people call them *irun didi*, but in the Caribbean, they're called canerows after the cane fields where the enslaved people were forced to work. In America, they call them cornrows after the corn fields."

Aniyah admired the pictures on the salon walls. One picture showed a woman, her hair wrapped in cloth, like how her mum would sometimes protect her tight curls.

"Who's that?" she asked.

EJ bounded over. "I know that one! That's Queen Nanny."

"That's right," smiled Joy. "She was captured in her homeland, Ghana, and brought to Jamaica as an enslaved person. She was a wise warrior queen who victoriously commanded the Maroons in the battle for their freedom."

Olivia's face lit up. "Mum's family came to London from Ghana! What's a Maroon?" she asked.

"The Maroons fought for their freedom and escaped enslavement in the Caribbean and built their own settlements. Queen Nanny led the Maroons up in Blue Mountain, in Jamaica," said Joy.

Yara nodded. "We had Maroons in South America too. Queen Nanny reminds me of King Zumbi and Gaspar Yanga."

"Who are *they*?" EJ asked.

"They formed settlements known as quilombos. King Zumbi led one of the most infamous quilombos in Palmares. They resisted capture in Brazil for almost a century," explained Yara.

"Yanga was an African man from Gabon, who led a Maroon settlement in Mexico."

Aunt Joy spun Aniyah around on the salon chair. "My next appointment will be here soon ... why don't you have a think about the style you want?"

Aniyah nodded.

"I brought the Ludi board from Blue Mahoes in case we had time," EJ said. "Let's play the game!"

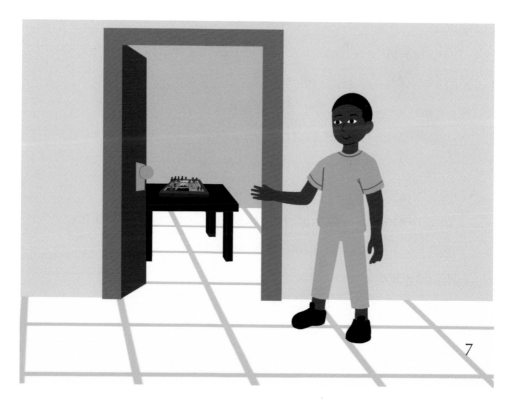

The game was a family heirloom with
magical properties. Etched on to the side were the words:

Roll double six, or double three,

let's learn about your history.

Every time they played, they were drawn into
an adventure!

When Aniyah finally rolled a double three, a puff of
iridescent smoke emitted from the board. A tornado that
formed a wormhole appeared and pulled them in.

Chapter 2

Olivia and EJ's faces came into view as Aniyah stepped through the dissipating fog.

"Aniyah, your hair!" said Olivia.

"*Your* hair has changed too," EJ told Olivia.

Aniyah and Olivia had canerows in their hair, braided into intricate patterns. Aniyah felt something rough against her neck.

"What is it?" asked EJ, peering at her.

"I'm not sure." Aniyah gripped the object between her fingers and prised it out. An iron charm dangled on a leather cord.

"It looks like a necklace," said Olivia.

"OK, so you two have fancy hair and we're in a jungle," said EJ, swatting away a mosquito.

Trees towered over them, and they were surrounded by lush, leafy plants. A choir of colourful birds fluttered up above, flitting from tree to tree. Aniyah tucked the necklace into the folds of fabric around her body.

"I think you're right," Aniyah said.

Suddenly, she froze.

EJ swung round and found himself face to face with a large snake!

"Let's get out of here!" Olivia cried. She pulled EJ backwards and the three of them ran through the dense jungle.

"Where *are* we?" Aniyah puffed. "And what year is it?"

"Why is it *so* hot?" EJ grumbled.

The Ludi board always brought them to a time in the past, and they usually arrived with to objects that helped them solve a problem.

Olivia patted the cloth draped around her body and shook her head. "I don't have anything."

EJ wasn't listening. "Did you see that?" he asked, edging closer to Aniyah and Olivia.

"See what?" asked Olivia.

"That tree moved!" replied EJ.

Aniyah and Olivia stared at the tree.

"Trees can't move," said Aniyah.

Suddenly, the leaves rustled, and a little monkey scuttled across a tree branch.

"See, it was just a monkey," laughed Olivia.

EJ frowned.

"Let's take a look around," said Aniyah.

"There! Did you see *that*?" cried EJ again.

Olivia shook her head. "No, nothing."

"The trees are watching us!"
EJ insisted. "EJ, stop playing around.
We've got to figure out where we
are," said Olivia, marching over to
a tree. She leant on its trunk; a lizard
scurried up the rough bark.

"Mr Tree, would you please tell
EJ that you don't have eyes."

"I don't have eyes,"
the tree thundered.

"Exactly! Now can we – "
Oliva froze.

"Olivia, watch out!"
shouted Aniyah.

Suddenly, the tree
grew arms and legs.
A giant hand
reached out.

"RUN!"
she screamed.

Aniyah desperately looked around. The roots of the trees surrounding them were huge; they twisted and knotted around each other to form a cage. The three of them were locked in!

In a panic, Olivia stumbled on a fallen branch and fell into the wet mud. She scurried backwards on all fours towards Aniyah and EJ. Giant tree figures loomed over them. Some of them had bows and arrows pointed in their direction!

"I wish we'd arrived with a bow and arrow," squirmed EJ.

"You wouldn't know what to do with it," Aniyah replied.

"I play computer games all the time ... right control stick and R2 duh!"

Aniyah, Olivia and EJ huddled back-to-back in a tight circle. EJ spotted a small opening – perhaps they could run through it and make their escape.

Aniyah picked up a stick from the ground and screamed, "Get back, I warn you!"

Another tree figure, perched on a branch above them, jumped down, closing the gap between the tree giants. He took the stick from Aniyah's hand and snapped it in two.

"Pfft … a stick, really?" said EJ.

"Well, it beats your square, L1, triangle whatever," replied Aniyah, crossly.

"Can you continue this when we're not about to be eaten by giant trees?" Olivia hissed.

The trees crowded closer.

Then an arm reached out and pulled down a mask to reveal a face. It was a man!

"Lower your weapons. It's only children and they have the map!" he called to the others. One by one, masks were removed.

"They're people in disguise," gasped Aniyah.

"I knew that," EJ said.

"We mean you no harm," said the man who'd first spoken. "I'm Benkos Biohó, and I lead this group. We don't have much time. Follow me!"

"What map? I thought you didn't find anything," EJ whispered, as they followed Benkos.

"I don't have a map," Aniyah whispered back.

"Me neither," said Olivia.

"We didn't mean to scare you. I wasn't expecting you so soon, and didn't realise you were young runaways. We were on a secret mission when I spotted you. We must take care," said Benkos, looking back at the children.

"Why?" asked EJ.

"You should know that in the Americas, people like us are under constant threat. The colonisers seek to destroy our communities and force us into enslavement," explained Benkos, ducking behind a tree.

"We're somewhere in America," gasped Olivia.

"Mmm probably in South America ... and they think we're runaways!" replied Aniyah, as they waded through a swamp.

"I'm not enjoying the South so far," EJ grimaced.

"What should I call you?" Benkos asked.

Aniyah swatted away more mosquitoes. "EJ, Olivia and Aniyah."

"I was like you once," Benkos said, "taken from my home against my will and forced to come to these lands here in New Granada. It was 1596 when we made our way down the Magdalena River, but the boat hit some rocks and sank. I tried to escape but was recaptured.

"My captors tried to strip me of my identity and call me 'Bozales'. But I'm not a Bozales, I'm a Mandinka from the kingdom of Kaabu," Benkos proudly proclaimed.

"In 1599 my wife, Wiwa and I, along with many others, rebelled against the oppressors. We escaped from Cartagena and fled into the swamps, then up into the mountains. For the last couple of years, we've been building our own communities in Arcabuco and living off the land, remaining hidden from outsiders."

"I think Benkos is a Maroon!" whispered Aniyah excitedly.

Olivia nodded. "And it must be about 1601."

"Until I find my way home, I'm the King of Arcabuco!" Benkos announced.

Chapter 3

"What's the secret mission?" EJ asked Benkos.

"Well, it wouldn't be a secret if I told you," Benkos replied.

"I suppose not," said EJ.

"Gold is abundant in the valley of Cauca – " began Benkos.

EJ's eyes lit up. "Is that the secret mission, looking for gold?"

"No," said Benkos. "People who've been enslaved are forced to pan for gold along the riverbeds that flow through Popayán, sifting through its sediments and washing its gold deposits for greedy miners.

"Efforts to pan for gold in Popayán have dwindled but some miners are on their way to Chisquio from the Port of Cartagena de Indias. They have some captured men with them, and we plan to rescue them. *That's* the secret mission."

"Where?" asked EJ.

Benkos pulled back the jungle foliage in front of them. "Right here!"

Aniyah, Olivia and EJ followed Benkos on to the trail. "We must act quickly. We've received word the miners will be here soon."

The Maroons began to chop into the trunk of a big tree until it toppled across the trail.

23

"Olivia and EJ, can you help block the path with anything else you can find. Aniyah, I'll need your help over there," Benkos directed.

EJ and Olivia worked together to lift a rock and placed it in front of the fallen trunk. Then they helped the others heave some logs on to the pile of rubble.

Aniyah looked up at the Maroons perched in the trees. They pulled down a thick, springy branch and Benkos reached up and grabbed it.

"Can you help me with this please, Aniyah?" Benkos gave her a long vine.

Benkos tied another vine to the branch. "Can you double knot this part? That's perfect. Now we cover this vine with lots of leaves."

"What now?" Aniyah asked.

"Now? Now we hide!" explained Benkos.

Aniyah, Olivia and EJ hid behind a tree. Everyone in the trees was camouflaged so well, they almost disappeared.

It seemed like they had been waiting forever, when suddenly, the jungle erupted into birdsong.

"It's like the birds are talking to each other," Olivia said.

Benkos smiled. "It's not the birds, it's us. It's how we communicate without being detected. That was the signal telling us to take position."

EJ made a shrieking noise. "How does my bird call sound?"

"You sound like a dying crow!" Aniyah said, covering her ears.

"Perhaps a little more practice," Benkos winced. "When we arrived here, the colonisers tried to stop us from speaking our language; they wanted us to forget our names and our identities. We were punished if we were caught speaking in our mother tongues. So, we came up with other ways to communicate, just like the map that led you to us in the swamp."

"The map?" asked Aniyah. She didn't have a map.

"The map in your hair, guiding us on this mission!" Benkos revealed. "The women started to communicate with their hair; they would use it as a way to plan escapes and draw maps."

Aniyah gasped as she began to trace a canerow in her hair with her finger, it wiggled like a snake.

"That's the river," explained Benkos.

Olivia felt the Bantu knot on her head.

"That's a mountain, and the thick braids indicate where the colonisers are," said Benkos.

Aniyah looked at EJ and Olivia. "We have maps in our hair!"

Another bird call travelled through the air; this time it was a lot closer. Suddenly, they heard hooves pounding the ground.

Chapter 4

Six men on horseback came into view. Stumbling along beside them was a line of men.

Aniyah felt an uneasy knot form in her stomach; the men on foot had chains around their wrists and waists.

The horseman at the front came to a halt. "STOP!" he yelled. "The path is blocked."

Five of the horsemen dismounted and walked up to the tree for a closer look.

When three of them stepped into the mound of leaves
Aniyah and Benkos had placed on the path, the giant
tree trunk sprung up. The vine on the ground tightened
around their ankles, and the horsemen flew up into
the air, screaming.

Benkos whistled like a bird. The Maroons in the trees threw large nets made of vines on to the men still on their horses below and jumped down on top of them. Aniyah, Olivia and EJ followed Benkos as he leapt out from behind the tree. As the last man still on his horse fumbled for his weapon, they heard the keys on his belt jingle.

Those keys look familiar, thought Aniyah.

More Maroons appeared, and they began to shoot arrows towards the last horseman.

The horseman ducked as an arrow brushed past his ear.
Desperately yanking at the reins, he turned his horse.

"GET HIM!" yelled Benkos, but it was too late.
The horseman had escaped. "He had the keys we needed
to unlock the chains!"

One of the horsemen they'd captured started to laugh.

"He'll be back with reinforcements! When they get
here, we'll capture you all, find your village and raze it to
the ground."

Benkos picked up a rock and began to pound it against the metal chains. Some of the enslaved people desperately tried to pull them off with their bare hands.

"It'll take forever to break through these chains; they'll have to come with us as they are," said one of Benkos' men.

"They won't be able to move around the jungle, Bamidele," Benkos replied.

Aniyah suddenly realised what they'd found around her neck earlier. The charm on the cord. "It's a key!" But when she felt around her neck, it wasn't there. She ran back into the jungle.

"Aniyah, what's wrong? What key?" asked Olivia, running to catch up.

"The necklace ... it's disappeared," Aniyah replied.

EJ appeared beside them. "What about a necklace?"

"I think it was a key, not a charm. A key on the cord we found in my hair, but now it's gone," cried Aniyah.

"Don't worry," said EJ. "We'll help you find it."

Olivia nodded. "But let's try and *not* get lost!"

"Or eaten by alligators," Aniyah added.

They began to search through the trees.

"I found it!" Olivia called.

Aniyah and EJ ran over. The leather cord was hanging from a branch.

"It must have fallen off." Aniyah prised it from the tangle. "Quick! Let's give it to Benkos."

They ran back to the main track.

Benkos clutched the key in his hand as he forced it into the keyhole on the iron chains.

There was a loud crank before the chain opened and fell to the ground.

"YESSS! You were right," Olivia laughed. "It *is* a key."

Benkos swiftly freed the others.

The man Benkos had just freed beckoned EJ over. "E seun a dúpé," he said.

"I don't understand," EJ said.

"It's our mother tongue," smiled Bamidele. "He's thanking us."

The man spoke again. "His name is Tayo," Bamidele continued. "But there's no time to talk. We must get out of here quickly."

Aniyah, Olivia and EJ followed the Maroons as they disappeared back into the swamp, leaving the miners swinging from the nets in the tree.

Sweat slid down their brows as they tried to keep up. Olivia was amazed at how the Maroons could effortlessly navigate their way around the trees. As Benkos pulled EJ over a giant tangled root, the men in front began shouting.

Chapter 5

"It's Tayo. He's been bitten!" said Bamidele.

"Look!" said Aniyah, pointing to the ground.

"Snake!" shrieked Olivia, as it slithered away.

EJ shuddered. "Not another one!"

Benkos took a closer look at Tayo. He was lying on the ground, writhing in pain. The other freed men were huddled together beside him; they looked scared and exhausted.

"It doesn't look good," said Benkos.

"How can we help him?" asked Aniyah.

"We must find a plant that will help draw out the venom," Benkos replied. "And quickly! Bamidele, you wait with Tayo. Aniyah, EJ and Oliva, come with me. The others can make their way back to our village," said Benkos.

"What does the plant look like?" asked Aniyah.

"Its leaves look like this." Benkos picked up a stick from the ground and began to draw into the soil. "It has bright yellow flowers shaped like this."

"Let's try over here," Olivia suggested.

Benkos, Aniyah, Olivia and EJ frantically searched for the plant Benkos had described. Eventually, they came to a shallow river with ragged rocks protruding from beneath its surface. Benkos waded through the water and guided the children one by one, using the rocks as a bridge.

"Be very careful," Benkos warned. "Step on to this rock over here, and then this one. Good."

When they'd all made it across the river safely, they began their search for the plant once more.

Aniyah ran her hand over a large, waxy leaf; she'd never seen anything like it. She bent down to feel the grooves and ridges of another. *This doesn't look like the plant we're looking for,* she thought.

"Over here, come quick! I've found it!" shouted EJ, poking his head through some large leaves.

"That's it! Now, collect the leaves," Benkos explained, "and I'll gather the roots."

Aniyah and EJ crouched down beside Olivia.

"That should do it," said Benkos. "Let's get out of here."

Aniyah felt her hair. "I know the way back! Just follow the maps."

"That's the river we crossed, and we must be over here," Olivia said, tracing her finger across one of Aniyah's canerows.

"Does that mean we go that way?" EJ said.

"Yes!" grinned Benkos. "Hurry."

When they arrived back, Bamidele was still by Tayo's side. Tayo's eyes were closed.

"Are we too late?" asked Olivia anxiously, as they handed over the leaves and roots.

"I hope not," said Bamidele. "Help me prepare the herbs."

Aniyah, EJ and Olivia crushed up the leaves and the roots and Bamidele rubbed them on Tayo's wound. "Now we must wait and see," he said.

"We'll rest here for the night; Bamidele and I will keep a lookout," nodded Benkos.

The next morning, Aniyah woke to a tug on her shoulder. Momentarily, she forgot where she was. "What is it, EJ?" she moaned.

"It's Tayo!" EJ replied.

"He's going to be OK!" said Olivia.

"Once we get back to our village, the doctor will see to him," said Bamidele, "but he's well enough to walk."

Benkos appeared; he looked like he'd been running. "The miner from yesterday is nearby, with a new group of men. Let's go!"

44

Time for another swamp trek, thought EJ, as he, Aniyah and Olivia followed the Maroons through the jungle.

They hadn't gone far before they heard the thunder of horses' hooves.

"Quick!" Benkos hissed. "Hide!"

Chapter 6

Benkos and Bamidele leapt over
the gigantic roots of a nearby tree, then
they helped the others to climb over.
Olivia's foot slipped on the rough
bark and got caught in between two
entangled roots.

"I'm stuck!" she cried.

The sound of hooves got closer
and closer.

Benkos managed to slip her foot
out just in time. They scurried beside
the others, into a dark opening beneath
the tree.

The horsemen stopped and everyone
held their breath.

"There's no one here," they heard one
of the men say. "Let's take another path."

They waited a short while after
the sound of hooves faded away.

Benkos poked his head out first.
"I think it's safe to continue our journey."

They trudged for hours and hours, using the information in Aniyah and Olivia's hair to avoid the groups of colonisers, until, at last …

"Welcome to our Palenque!" said Benkos. "Our home, Arcabuco."

"I can see some houses," Olivia said.

Aniyah ran a hand over her hair. *All the trails leading to the village are mapped in our hair*, she thought. *Everything leads here.*

A woman unearthing yams was singing, and the other villagers were singing back in response.

Chickens roamed free, pecking at insects, as men, women and children worked the land. A man held the reins attached to a mule pulling a plough, and children pounded the soil with long sticks. Women filled woven baskets with pineapples, bananas, mangos, guavas and papayas.

"Tatá! You're back," a voice cried.

"Orika," said Benkos, "I'd like you to meet Aniyah, Olivia and EJ."

"Hello," said Orika.

"This is my daughter; she'll show you around and prepare you for the feast. Tonight, we must celebrate!"

49

Orika led Aniyah, EJ and Olivia around the village. An old woman was sitting on a log surrounded by the village children. She was using a stick to draw pictures in the earth.

"We teach the younger children the customs, traditions and tongue of our forefathers so we never forget who we are," smiled Orika.

They passed a hut where a girl and two boys were weaving dried grass into the roof.

"Can I help?" asked EJ.

"Of course," Orika replied. "Aniyah and Olivia, come with me. We can start unbraiding the maps from your hair."

They sat in the shade while a group of women began to loosen the braids out of Aniyah's and Olivia's hair using wooden combs.

"You've got more than maps in your hair!" Orika smiled.

"We have?" Aniyah replied. Orika held out her hand. There, in the middle of her palm, was a gold nugget!

As the women continued, they found more gold and seeds for different crops.

"We'll be able to plant these seeds to grow more crops and exchange the gold for livestock and goods," Orika told them.

That night, the moon looked like the skin of the drums the Maroons were playing. They hammered out a beat as everyone in the village danced and sang.

"Nice hair," EJ said, looking at Olivia and Aniyah.

"Who's that dancing?" Aniyah wondered.

"It's Benkos!" said Olivia.

Benkos removed his mask. The feathers and beads on his clothing swung around him as he danced.

As the children began to jump up and down to the beat of the drums, a tornado that formed a wormhole appeared and pulled them in.

They were back at Kisanu.

Aunt Joy popped her head around the door.

"I'm free now; do you know what you want yet, Aniyah?"

Aniyah felt her hair, it was back in a big, thick, loosed-out afro.

"Yes," she nodded. "And I *will* sit still."

She described the hairstyle she wanted, and Aunt Joy worked her magic.

MAPS AND MESSAGES

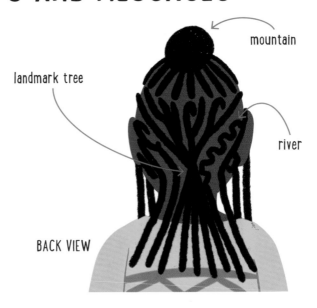

mountain

landmark tree

river

BACK VIEW

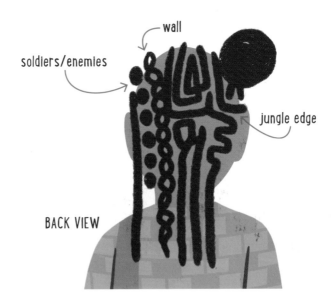

wall

soldiers/enemies

jungle edge

BACK VIEW